The Promise

The Promise

A Novella

Maria I. Hodges

Cumberland House
Nashville, Tennessee

Published by Cumberland House Publishing, Inc., 431 Harding Industrial Drive, Nashville, Tennessee 37211.

Story and illustrations: Maria Isabel Hodges
Cover design: Karen Phillips
Text design: Mary Sanford

Library of Congress Cataloging-in-Publication Data
Hodges, Maria I., 1948–
The promise : a novella / Maria I. Hodges.
p. cm.
ISBN 1-58182-017-8 (alk. paper)
I. Title.
PS3558.034342P76 1999
813'.54--dc21 98-55227
CIP

Printed in the United States of America
1 2 3 4 5 6 7—05 04 03 02 01 00 99

To my son,
Charles Sean McManus

Contents

Introduction

THIS WILL BE my eighty-first Easter and the last I shall spend with my treasured journal.

It is fitting, I suppose, that Charlotte was the one who asked for it more than twenty years after I first read it to her and to the children of the mission. Her request, though surprising at first, is one I gladly grant.

I've chosen pure white tissue paper, now wrapping the journal carefully. The book needs no other adornment. The story alone is the gift I am passing to Charlotte for her own children and to carry on my work at the mission.

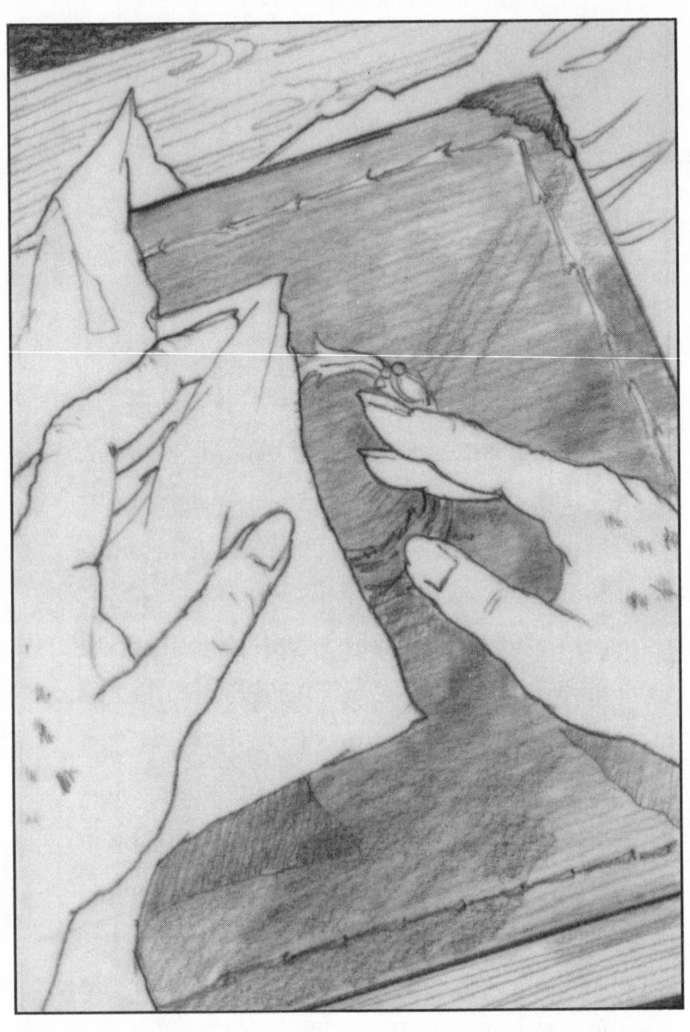

I've chosen pure white tissue paper, now wrapping the journal carefully.

The sun is setting now and long fingers of deep shadow creep into my home. Charlotte will be here in less than an hour. Through the dim light I see my hands tremble as I tuck the crisp paper around the leather binding. My eyes are misting—whether from joy or sadness at the journal's departure I do not know.

This moment was long in coming.

I have waited for this day from the first Easter I brought the journal to the mission. I have always hoped that one of my children would remember the story through the years and hold it fast to her heart.

My dearest wish now is that the promise of the story will last through the generations of Charlotte's family; as my own childless lineage is now coming to an end.

The Promise

We Begin

Standing squarely on the corner of 10th and West Haven streets is the largest of three missions that serve the community of Atlanta's poor and homeless.

The building used to be a department store warehouse, and as such, it is stone-faced and imposing. Inside, it is usually cold and uninviting—even in the spring, the time I now think of as I wait for Charlotte.

Three times a year, however, the largest room is gaily decorated and the word is spread, inviting those in need to dine.

Hundreds come through the doors of the mission every holiday.

We often wondered where they ate and were attended to on days other than on the special feasts of Thanksgiving, Christmas, and—my favorite—Easter.

When all of us gathered, celebrating that Sunday, the children gingerly approached our table set with ham dinners and clung to their mothers. The shyest and smallest had to be coaxed to eat, but once they relaxed, they soon giggled and laughed with the other children as if they were cousins sharing a family picnic on a warm July afternoon.

Retirement from my career as a teacher brought me this new pleasure of giving to others.

Teaching in the public schools had been an excellent way for me to be a surrogate mother, and I never felt for a moment the void left in my life by not marrying and bearing children.

The time of courtship and marriage arrived at a stage in my life when I was too busy caring for my aging parents, and when they died I was left with only their abundant goods and the emptiness of this mansion in Virginia Highlands.

I had been born in this same house during my parents' twenty-fifth year as a married couple.

Maybe because I had come into their lives so late, I was indulged shamelessly.

Or maybe both my father and mother realized when I was born that I would outlive them by decades and would need all the love they could lavish on me to last a lifetime of memories.

In either case, I was in my thirties when

they finally died after long illnesses. My father passed away first, and my mother joined him a scant two years later. They left me this wonderful house that is filled with memories.

By then I was too independent to see the value in sharing my life with anyone, and I had no desire to do so.

I was consumed with acquiring an education that would allow me to make myself useful to the community.

Teaching had been an easy decision to make since I wanted to follow in my mother's footsteps.

Although she lacked the formal education that would have given her the same career I later chose, her natural talents led the neighborhood to depend upon her for the lessons of the hearth.

She was the one who taught my childhood friends how to knead dough and baste a savory chicken.

My parents could well afford the help to accomplish these tasks for them, but my mother preferred caring for us herself, and her skills were well known in the neighborhood. The mothers brought their girls into our home, all of them learning first hand what upper crust Southern cooking should taste like.

My father had made his fortune in the insurance business, and my earliest memories of him were of his attempts to explain the principles of life expectancy and the like.

Memories of my mother center on the holidays and her elaborate dinners and our joy-filled home at Thanksgiving, Christmas, and Easter.

Thanksgiving was centered on food and

the company of friends celebrating the blessings of our lives. We had many, for my father prospered in business and both my mother and he spent deliciously on the pleasures of our home.

At Christmas, my father took me to the hills outside of Atlanta, choosing and cutting the perfect sapling for our front room.

We placed it in our home and decorated it with all the care we could bestow upon it.

I still have many tattered boxes of ornaments from those days, and although I rarely take the time now to raise a tree in that same room, when I do I am transported back to that happy time. I cherish memories of my father placing the golden paper star on the topmost branch and my mother's honey cake filling our home with the familiar scent of cinnamon and brown sugar.

I still have many tattered boxes of ornaments from those days. . . .

But my favorite of all holidays was Easter.

On that day my mother once again prepared a feast. My parents invited all who could fit at our large oak table.

She set the table with the fine china, crystal, and silver of her native England. We feasted on cloved ham, roasted sweet potatoes, fresh baked breads, and her homemade ice cream.

Afterward, the small crowd gathered around her, hearing the story she read from our heirloom journal.

The questions that followed her reading were always the same, even though her answers and the listeners never varied.

All who heard the story wished to learn about the history of the writer once they realized that it was written as an observation of a story all of us knew well.

My mother would only smile, saying that her own father had given her the book so that she could continue to share the story and that we should concentrate on the message rather than the messenger.

She never attempted to explain who the writer was to them, nor did she ever confide in me if she knew.

Nevertheless, the story was enjoyed by all who heard it, and each year we waited to hear it again, as if new clues could be gleaned from each fresh telling.

When my parents died, the same people crowded into my home every Easter even though, since I was alone, I had no desire to prepare the traditional feast.

They simply expected the story to be reread. Through the years, the children grew, married and still returned, bringing their own families to hear the tale.

After a time the other holidays seemed too empty when I had to spend them by myself, so on the first year after I had left my employment I sought the company of others again.

Choosing to spend my holidays with those who were less fortunate than myself, I was led to the large mission directly in the shadow of the luxurious hotels of the center city.

At first my involvement with the mission had been self-serving. I stepped, from my home laden with all the comforts one can accumulate in a lifetime, into a world I thought would provide distraction and break the solitude of special days.

I had no connection with the poor and homeless who came to feast upon what I had prepared.

The first year, working among them, I

noticed the little things that their dignity probably blinded them to: the ill-fitting shoes, clothes that were too large and faded, and the hands of the older women that were gnarled and worn with the hard work they had endured. I had no insight into their lives until I talked with them and could admire what they had accomplished and how they cared for their families with such few resources.

By the second year they were giving me more than I ever could return in material pleasures of food and drink. They showed me how they overcame hardships and instilled in their families an appreciation for the basic truths of life.

It was destined that my journal would make its way into their midst, hopefully further inspiring and nurturing their children.

They fit together well, the story and the listeners, as if they were made for one another from the beginning of all time. In a way I suppose they were, for the story is of the promise that gives us the knowledge we are worthy of great love and sacrifice.

It is the story of Easter.

* * *

THE EASTER SUNDAY I met Charlotte was the second year I gave my time to the mission.

By then I knew from talking with the women that many were alone with their children and depended upon us for the small charities we offered a few times a year: a meal, a place to forget their world for a day, and the boxes of canned goods, rice, beans, and flour we gave them.

The first Easter I spent at the mission, I was given the task of entertaining the children while their mothers relaxed for a while. My job was a spur of the moment decision made by necessity and need, and ill-prepared though I was, I carried it well.

On the second Easter, the one to which I now turn my attention, I brought my beloved journal in order to read to the children as they sat waiting patiently for what I had to offer them.

Their faces had all been carefully washed, their hair combed, braided, and bowed. They were clothed in the best they had. I sat in the middle and asked my group of tiny strangers if any of them would first like to draw near enough to see my book up close.

Only one came—the boldest, and later I would know her as the most intelligent—my dear Charlotte.

She came to my side, a shy and silent six-year-old, and touched the ancient leather binding. . . .

She came to my side, a shy and silent six-year-old, and touched the ancient leather binding with her small forefinger, tracing the carved leaves and flowers on the cover and the name Sara in gold on the spine. When she asked about its origin, I gave the same answer I usually gave to neighborhood children and friends who had seen it—that the book had always been in my family.

It came from ages ago and from a long forgotten source. Only the story on its fragile pages remained to be read and reread—especially on Easter.

That is how we began, Charlotte and I.

The mystery of the journal drew us together from the very beginning.

The Journal

THIS IS THE story I shared with the children of the mission.

Though the original will now be in the care of Charlotte so that she can continue sharing it this year and in future years with my charges—and with the new ones who will come through those doors—I would like to think that the story has such merit that it is worthy of being shared with others as well.

When my own mother first read it to me, besides being curious about the writer, I asked her of the truth behind the story.

You may have the same question. So I

shall give you the answer that my mother gave me so long ago.

Sometimes there are simply things we do not understand about this world and most assuredly about the world beyond this one.

We are free to choose what to believe in, and in making our choices we find our own paths and realize our destinies. Hopefully, the story of the journal will guide us to the truth.

Now I shall let the words of the journal and the story of the promise stand on its own.

The Birth

We were in the longed for city and the night had finally come. The air was clear and warm, and stars glowed in the sky as from the beginning. I remember that time. The great hand swept across the ocean of darkness and created the light from nothing.

The sheer thought of light in the darkness brings tears to my eyes now as I think of it.

I weep thinking of the generous love He has given in creating it. He demanded that there be the greatness of fire in the sky and around the depths of the regions we have traveled in for so long in darkness, alone until now. When He decided that there would be the ones we call the others, He created the light to lead them on their way. To energize and renew. To give them hope and a way to exist and thrive.

The great hand swept across the ocean of darkness and created light from nothing.

This light was and is a great blessing. Perhaps the greatest of the blessings that He has given until this time, or that I can remember He has given. For I have not always been with Him.

I was an image that came after the surge of the army that sought to destroy Him. I was created out of the need to fill the void left by the ones who were sent to the far regions and to the punishment of never seeing His face again.

I took my place by His side, honoring and adoring Him as was my duty and privilege.

I observed all that He directed from His loving heart.

I must now start with the story of the birth of His Son. Though many centuries have passed since that time, my memories are as clear as if it were only moments ago.

* * *

The time drew near and I had been sent to summon those who had anticipated the birth and awaited His arrival as I had. We had been waiting for ages, from the beginning of my creation and the creation of those in the East. I journeyed to the region and brought with me ten thousand more to add to the ten thousand who had seen the two travel on their way to the city.

We came in haste and prepared ourselves for the birth as we traveled through the firmament.

We purified our hearts and cast our thoughts only to Him who would come tonight.

The descent to the city was long, and on the way I drew Him near to my heart and reassured Him that He was loved even

The descent to the city was long, and on the way I drew Him near to my heart. . . .

before I had seen Him. He had known of me before my existence, and loved me and created me. I gave this back to Him in full measure before I saw His face and adored Him from my place in His new life.

The One who has created the light has promised Him to the others, and in His promise He has released the others from the blame of what is to come. It is a sadness we all bear. We do not know what is to happen, but we know that it will be a tragedy and those who will cause it will forever pay for it, maybe not in the world they know now, but in the One that will come.

Then He will have to be sent again to undo the chaos of the times and the destruction of what He created. But I go too far—now is the time for joy and to tell you of His coming.

We took our places by her side, a distance

away so as to give her privacy but not so far as to leave her abandoned in her final hour. Our leaders have come on their own, for the Great One has told them long before of the exact hour and place of His birth.

The mother comforted her companion and bid him lay by the door to guard them in the night, and there he fell asleep. We were struck by the gentleness with which she whispered to him in his sleep, reassuring him that all is well and to dream on without the fear of the world on his shoulders.

Many times in their travels to the city he had been overcome with the responsibility of caring for her, as she was great with the One who is to come. We who had been chosen to guard her as part of her army had been allowed to serve them with sweetmeats and fresh fruits on their way and he has offered his gratitude to the Great One.

This was little enough to do for him, and we looked forward to the time when we could do more, though that time may never come.

We watched her as she cleaned the room with her own hands and swept the floor for His arrival, preparing a suitable place for His birth.

The room was small and although we trusted the Great One, we wondered in our deepest thoughts why He allowed Himself—the part of Himself that will come from the mother—to be born here in this place. But I tried to think not what this means in His life. I put the thought from my mind and watched and waited for the moment that was coming.

We knew the time was near when the leaders moved to her side and closed in on her, shielding her from our sight. I drew into myself at the moment out of the fear of seeing the birth we had longed for so long. It must happen as the Great One has said, yet once it did, it would change the world forever.

The first sound of His voice came through the air clear and bright as if His words were written centuries before. He spoke with clarity though His age defied this miracle. As I looked below, I saw the mother reaching for Him from the hands of the leader of leaders, and the tears flowed from my being.

He was born.

His was one with the world.

He has finally come and will live as one of the others until He fulfills the promise and is called back to where He was created, out of that part of the Great One that loves the others with the power of eternity.

Joy was felt throughout the crowd of the multitude in the room and we raised our voices to proclaim our love for the One who has come. The sounds of this beautiful harmony cannot be described here in my humble hand.

It was like the sound of instruments and voices all at once, and the harmony flowed into itself as water mixes with wine. In all the centuries of my existence in the world of the others, I have never heard sounds such as those. I hold them in my heart as part of my dearest memories of Him and look back at the time of His birth when I feel the deepest sadness at being parted from His sight.

Now, in the still of the night while I write this passage, I wonder if the world as it was created can ever be appreciated by the others and cherished for what it is.

It has been torn and destroyed, as He was, and now only the remnants of the earth are left. We exist as if in limbo for the time when it shall be renewed. It shall, of that I can be assured. For the Great One would not have conceived of its worthiness had He not had a plan for its end. Years after His birth I learned from Him that it will end gloriously rather than in shame.

When the One had finally come, when the moment His birth had arrived, we of the legions were bathed in the utmost feeling of elation. It cannot be described. There are no words from this or any other language that can tell the full story of the emotion that each of us felt at the time of His coming.

We knew at the instant of His birth that the legions of the others would never forget Him, that His life would be forever chronicled, and we were right.

The world could have stopped at that instant, so perfect was its salvation merely by His coming, but the Great One had His own plan for the fulfillment of the promise.

At the time of His birth, it was hidden from us.

I wonder now, as I write this, if it was hidden from the mother as well.

Would she have consented to His coming if she had known what was to happen? But she gave of herself, freely choosing to accept the role of motherhood to the Father's Son.

We of the air were overcome with love and adoration at the sight of Him. The time of His birth was the single most important event of my existence, and if I seem to dwell on this it is because I know that I shall never be allowed to see it again.

He will come again, as the others hope He will and as it is ordained, but I will not be present in my form of today nor of yesterday.

The hour of His birth passed. He was now safely of the world, and the leaders stood by the mother's side and watched while she wrapped Him in the clean linen cloths she had brought with her for His comfort.

The One who was waited for slept with His tiny fist up to His precious mouth and slipped one small thumb between His pursed lips. He would progress as one of the others, slowly and with the growth of months and years, finally taking on the abilities of those who care for Him.

The mother sat by His side and watched over Him throughout the long night, and we continued singing above her head and lulled Him to sleep with our songs.

She heard us now, as she was often

The mother sat by His side and watched over Him throughout the long night, and we continued singing above her head. . . .

allowed to do, and saw us in the room. The Great One gave her the comfort of seeing legions with her during the night, keeping her from the fear of being alone with only her companion for protection.

The hours passed slowly. At the deepest part of the night the air became cold and the mother took the veil from her hair and placed it carefully over the infant.

The Great One looked down upon her there with His Son and gave us the power of warming the room. We each in unison breathed on the pair, and the air around her became more comfortable as she and her Son rested on into the night.

Toward the end of the night, the mother lay her head on the rock near the infant's shelter and slept for a few hours while still listening for the evenness of His breathing, as if to reassure herself that He was really hers.

This was the time we had waited for. The Great One had long ago ordained that her dreams would be the place where we could commune with her, and now it was our turn to adore her and love her.

Each of us, in our own way, spoke to her heart and told her how much we loved what she had done for the world and for us.

The mother responded in her dreams, lifting her spirit to us where we brought her to the Great One, who greeted her with all the joy of a father to a cherished child.

He had seen her grow and mature through her years in the temple and in her promise to her companion. Now she had carried His Son well and had delivered Him there in the room below, by herself, with only the leaders in attendance.

He was proud of her tonight and gave her the blessing of the ages which had been reserved for her for the day she would give birth. From the moment the world was created, He had reserved the blessing for the night His promise became flesh, and He gave it freely and without reservation.

Her spirit responded in kind, thanking Him for the great honor that had been given her and rededicating herself to His honor and glory.

When the morning sun began to rise over the mountains, her spirit returned to the world and to her body, which rested below. The instant her spirit descended to the world she awoke and turned her attention to the One who had come.

He awoke as the rays of sun spread into the rough room, and He was immediately hungry, as an infant of that tender age would be.

She took Him from the place where He

slept and cleaned Him, drawing Him near her so that He could find the nourishment He wanted. We hid our faces again, giving the child and His mother the solitude they needed.

The child finished and raised His tiny voice, signaling His arrival to the companion and awaking him. The man went into the room, looked at the infant, and knelt in adoration.

He fell prostrate on the dirt floor, stretching his arms in front of him, thanking the Great One who had seen them safely to the city, and for the pleasure of allowing him to see the sight of the child before him. He also thanked Him for the passing of the night and the health of the mother.

The child raised His tiny fingers to the companion, then returned them to His side. We looked on the scene of those below us and wondered if the child could now have some of the insight that He was destined to have in His later years.

Did He recognize the man and the woman, and was this a blessing for them both? Or was this the gesture of a child in His first hours of life, and would He now live as one of the others, without the powers of the Great One, until He was ready to take His place as a leader in their midst?

The Great One kept the answers to these secrets from us. We only knew that He had finally come and had taken the form we now saw below. It had been ordained from the beginning, and now the time had come. We raised our voices again to the Great One for allowing it to come to pass and for His generosity to the world of the others in sending this part of Himself to them.

Now it was time for the man to leave the

room, tending to the wants of the mother. She bid him farewell in her quiet way, never conversing much with him. But when she did it was with dignity and love.

The companion went out into the city, finding food for her nourishment while she was in the room and for their trip back to their home. While He was gone, the mother tended the child, comforting Him and warming Him with the feel of her own body.

When the man returned, he had with him food enough to last the long days he knew the mother and her son would spend there in the room before they would travel on. Later, when they needed more, he went out into the city, trading the goods he had brought to feed them, and in this way he provided the mother with fresh fruits and bread and she was made comfortable and freed from the worry of providing for herself.

On the third night after the birth, those who had come from the East were summoned from the site and I was taken to the Great One for His blessing and to hear His wishes.

It was that night that I was given charge of the One who had come.

The Great One told me to never leave His side.

He said that I would be a special one of the legion, guarding Him for His life from now on during the time He was among the world of the others.

I was overcome with joy at this news, for it was what I had wanted but dared not ask of the Father. Yet it was freely given as if I had petitioned for it from the beginning of my creation.

I sang His praises that night and lifted my voice in His presence, proclaiming His mercy and goodness when He chose me for this sacred duty among all the others of my legion.

I returned to the family below and saw that the mother was sleeping. I entered her dreams and showed her that I would be with her son always and that I would help her care for Him and watch over Him.

When she heard my thoughts, she thanked me and told me how much it meant to her knowing that I would be with her and that she was very glad her son would have me in His life. At dawn she awoke, and I began my first day as the child's guardian.

In the morning the companion provided more nourishment for the mother and talked with her while she tended the child.

The day passed quickly, and the night soon came again.

At the first hour of darkness three strangers came to the door, asking if this was the place where they had been led, even though they did not know that the legions of the Great One had been leading them to this place.

They were dazed and unsure of their request or why they had been sent.

The companion knew why they were at the doorway, and he let them into the room, telling them this was the child they were seeking.

The strangers were dressed in worn clothing as if they spent their days outside in the rains and winds. They fell on their knees in the room and talked to the mother in low voices while proclaiming their love for her child, all the while not fully understanding the complete mystery of the sight.

The visit lasted for a few hours, and the mother and her companion offered them fresh bread and a few pieces of dried fish. At the end of their visit, the companion and the mother thanked them for their good wishes and bid them safe travel back to their home in the mountains.

The mother then turned her attention to the One who had come, caring for Him and tending to His needs.

I took up my place by her side, as I was allowed to do, and looked on her and the child with love. I adored Him all the more in my heart.

I weep now, as I write this, when I think back and remember what happened to the dearest of the dear, our precious child and the continuance of the Great One. How He suffered and what pain He endured for those who knew Him not.

There, in the small room of His birth, He was but a small child beginning His life with the love and protection of the man and the mother. Just these two, and not the multitude of the others He deserved to know Him and care for Him.

This was the way the Great One had ordained, and although I wondered what plan there was in the future of the child at the time of His birth, I questioned not the way that He was born, not then nor now—many centuries after His coming.

Childhood

I remember with fondness and love the first years of the Son of the Great One's life.

At this time I was still in my ethereal

form, and I existed in the heavens in the presence of the Great One.

Now as I write these words, bound as I am by this body of the others and committed to the new charge of sharing the purpose of my dear one's life with all those who would hear the message, I cherish memories of the time I watched over His days as a child of the earth.

As I have said in the story of His birth, He came from the spirit of the Great One. The legions of the air rejoiced at His coming and I, above all, was chosen to be by His side—guiding Him in His days of growth and life among the others.

When He was a child, His last days were hidden from me.

If the Father of us all had revealed to me what was to befall His Son, I would have trembled at the sight of Him from the beginning of my duties and been fearful all the days of His life.

Yet, because I was innocent of His destiny, only knowing that His greatness would be one day revealed to the others in a way not open to me, I was blinded to His fate and served Him daily in wonder and love.

I delighted in the simplest of His efforts.

The smile on His tiny face. The way His eyes sought out the newness of the earth and the gestures of His hands and feet.

The Son of the Great One grew in beauty and grace.

During His first year, He learned how to speak to His mother, the delight of His life, without words—giving His affection and love with the soft murmurings of babyhood.

I rejoiced in seeing Him progress from an infant to a small child, the image of His fos-

ter father. His mother, whom the Great One had chosen from the beginning of time to tend His Son in His earthly incarnation, adored Him and worshiped Him, for she knew from whence He had come and what His true nature was.

When the mother and her companion tended the child, they did so with great reverence, handing the Son to one another on bended knee and lowering their eyes from the radiance of His beauty.

The child grew through the months and years as a normal child of the times—crawling, then toddling, and finally walking to His mother's arms with confidence.

In those early years, He discovered the world around Him—the wind, the rain, flowers, trees, and birds of the sky.

All this was new to Him, as to any other child of the world, for His true Father had so ordained that He grow in stature as one of the world and not as One who had come from the eternal heavens of His first and last home. My own happiness was immeasurable during the time of His childhood.

I delighted in seeing Him grow through the years as if I were His mother.

In my own way I saw Him as my child. I thought of Him as my own son to treasure and care for as if I alone had borne Him and would see Him grow to manhood.

The mother was an extension of myself, a worldly being who could hold Him when I could not, who could touch His sweet face and stroke His fine baby hair when I was denied the chance to reach out and feel the treasure that was hers.

But all this I hid, in my secret heart, from the Father of us all, lest He deem that I was becoming too close to the Son. I dared not

reveal to the others my attachment to the Son, nor my great love of Him.

I existed in two dimensions during the time of His childhood. The first was as a guardian of the One who had come, delighting in watching over His growth and fearful at each misstep that He would come to injury or harm.

I became like His mother, my ethereal form only a manifestation of love and adoration of the child.

The second dimension of my existence was as a being who wished dearly that I could manifest myself for only one second, one instant that it would take to reach out and hold Him for the moment it would take to announce my love and proclaim that I was forever His.

I never knew if He sensed my presence near Him during this time. I dearly wished that He would know that I was near, but I dared not petition the Great One to reveal this to His Son. I wished to remain as a guardian, delighting in the duties I was given, if only as a watcher and trusted servant of the Father.

To the mother, I remained her faithful protector, and she always knew I was with her as I was still permitted to reveal myself to her in the dreamworld.

I was able to show her that I was near her in spirit and that I was close to her in times of tribulation that may visit her during her great duty of raising the child.

Her singular dignity and closeness to the Great One prevailed, and she turned to Him when in doubt and only needed me to proclaim that I was near.

The small family was supported by the simple duties of the foster father and he

provided well for them with the toil of His hands. Their days were spent in the activities of the times, undistinguished from the other families of the town in which they lived, for so ordained the Great One that His Son grow in body as one of their world.

The child continued to prosper all the days of His life until His twelfth year on earth.

It was during this year that my greatest sorrow of His childhood came about, and thinking of it now pierces my heart as I write these words.

I shall relate the event as I can remember, and in writing I shall leave out nothing of the time that brought me such anguish.

The family was of the world, as I have said, and as such were travelers to the holy city to worship and make sacrifices during the time of the year known as the feast of the unleavened breads, as required during that time.

The companion traveled alone during two of the feasts, but on the third he brought the mother and child.

They worshiped for the seven days of the feast. At the end of the feast it was time to return to their home, and the crowd of travelers left the city, the men and women separately.

The companion and the mother both thought that the Son was with the other, and His absence was not discovered until the night of the first day's journey from the city.

The mother's sorrow at the loss of the Son was the greatest pain of her life to that day.

She and the companion sought the child in the paths of the desert from the city. The night was thick, and only the stars and moon guided them back to the city.

I knew the Son was safe, though I was prevented from telling the mother. The Son, my treasure, was deep in the city.

He lifted those who were afflicted with sorrows of the spirit, and turned their thoughts to the One who had sent Him.

On the second day, the mother wondered aloud to her companion if the child had been lost on the way to the city of His birth. It was then that the Great One spoke to her heart and led her back to the city of the feast to search among the townspeople.

The two people found the trail of the child and followed Him to the temple. There the leaders were in discussion about the coming of the Messiah, and the child was with them, deep in the talk with His elders.

There the leaders were in discussion about the coming of the Messiah, and the child was with them, deep in the talk with His elders.

The mother was overjoyed at finding her son, and yet she was confused as to why He had wounded her so in finding His way from her sight.

He responded to her admonishments that He must be about His Father's business. The meaning of His words was not immediately revealed to her, but she fell upon Him with sweet kisses as the elders told her of His great wisdom and questioned her at length about His training and studies.

She was too modest to respond, and instead of taking in the pride of their words, she held her love for her son in her heart and led Him from the temple with the companion in attendance.

All this I saw in my role as His guardian. I was present in the temple with Him and with the mother and companion as they

searched the city for their child. I was able to see all of them at the same time as a power given to me by the Great One.

Although I longed to console the mother, it was not of my role, and I suffered with her just as if I was of the earth and had lost my own dear child.

The child, the mother, and her companion returned to their home and took up their lives again as if nothing had happened to mar their tranquil lives.

In the mother's dreams I saw the loss of those three days and her wonder about the fate of her child when He was finally to be taken from her. For even in the early days of His youth, the mother knew that the Great One had a plan for her son.

This was not revealed to her clearly nor in any form but a mother's insight into her child's life. She felt a great weight when she

cared for the child from the day He was lost in the city.

It was a time to remind her that He was not to be hers forever. He belonged to the destiny the Great One had for Him, and it was her role to be only His mother and raise Him in virtue and love during the days she had with Him.

The child progressed and grew through His years in obedience to His mother and the companion, treating them equally and with devotion.

He learned the trade of His foster father and the value and use of the tools of working with the wood that grew on the low hills.

Together they fashioned useful forms for the homes of their town and together were sought out by the townspeople for their craftsmanship and their honor.

Their lives took on a rhythm of closeness

and calm, the mother keeping the home and the companion watching over the health and comfort of them all.

The child was always a model of perfect spiritual growth at the time of His youth and through the grace of His earthly parents continued to grow in stature and inner beauty.

Through His mother's teachings He learned the life of prayer and of communion with the Great One, His true Father.

Now as I look back over the time I was permitted to see Him as a youth, I am thankful again that the Great One allowed me to be present during this time.

The Promise Fulfilled

I watched with the mother as she raised the child and cherished Him all of His days.

When He became a man, He left the mother's side and bid the companion farewell.

He journeyed to the far lands, bringing the words of peace and love.

The foreign towns and cities contained a danger to the One who had come, and I stayed by His side, watching over Him. I saw the signs of anger in the others, as the elders began talking about His good works and raging against Him out of fear and jealousy.

I knew the end was drawing near, but the exact time was hidden from me.

The words of the ancients foretold His coming, yet they knew Him not as He walked among them.

He showed himself to be the Son of the Great One, yet they closed their eyes to Him and waited for another.

The elders wished to keep their place

among the others, for reason of riches and jewels, and they did not see what was before them—the One who had come was unadorned, yet His power was greater than theirs.

When the One who had come showed His power to the elders, they grew jealous and saw their own power lessen in the eyes of those who followed them.

When the elders spoke of the rules of their own power, they drove fear into the hearts of the people.

The One who had come spoke of the great love of the One who had sent Him, all the while trusting that the people would see Him for who He was.

His followers became many, and His every word was talked about in the cities where He visited.

A few of the more devoted traveled with

Him through the lands, seeking alms and begging with Him for their daily nourishment.

And so it was that the One who had come broke bread on the feast day with His chosen ones, and it was the last time they were together in one place.

The legions of the air were present, and I took my special place by His side and heard His last words to the devoted gathering.

There was one at the table whose heart was dark, who longed to grow in power and riches. The One who had come knew him for what he was and let him do the deeds that would lead to the death of them both.

My heart grows cold now as I think of Him at the table watching and waiting for the time He would act.

When the feast was over, my dear one left

with a few of His chosen ones and went out into the garden on the low mountain.

The Great One drew back the legions of the air but left me by His side as always. The Son talked to His Father in the darkest part of the night, and His words are still found among the books of the others as they remember this time.

He cried out, "O, my Father, if it is possible, let this cup pass from me, not as I will, but as you will."

He knew in His heart what was to come, and when I heard His words, I, too, knew the meaning of this time.

The end of the life of the One who had come was drawing near.

I ascended to the heavens to the throne of the Father and wept with tears that knew no bounds.

That death of the body would ever touch

my dear one was too painful to accept, yet the Great One proclaimed it as the way He had chosen to show His great love for those who walked the earth and waited for eternal life with Him.

And when He spoke of it as a way He had chosen, He also meant that the One who had come had chosen the course as well.

The promise had been given and would not be broken.

I fell prostrate at the feet of the Great One and waited for the words that would change my fate. I knew that the time had come for my duties to the Son to end, though I dearly wished to continue serving the Great One and His Son.

Because I had been with Him from the beginning and had known Him all the days of His life, and knew also that He came from the Father, the one true source of all in

I fell prostrate at the feet of the Great One and waited for the words that would change my fate.

heaven and on earth, the Great One charged that I proclaim all of my knowledge to any of the others who would open their hearts to the message.

How shall I do this? I asked, for I was without earthly form and had no power of speech the others could hear.

It was then that the Great One made it known to me that my life would be forever as one of the others on the earth in order to fulfill my new duties. I would take on their form and looks and walk the ground as they did until the end of time, though I would never age.

I would eat what they ate. Sleep as they slept. Dream as they dreamed. Yet I could keep my powers of good, that they sustain me in times of trial.

The one thing I could not do was prevent death.

As He spoke His last words to me, I spun to the ground in essence and pure soul and became flesh, inflamed with my new desire to please the Father and bring His message and the story of His Son to all who would listen.

I fled to the side of my precious charge.

So great was the pain in His heart that I hid from His sight, yet He knew I was there and noticed me in the shadows.

He continued His prayer to His Father, talking to the Great One again, lifting His spirit as He said, "O my Father, if this cup cannot pass away from me unless I drink it, your will be done."

Tears flowed from my soul and from my heart and the new body I had been given suffered the pain of knowing what was coming.

I reached out my hand to console Him,

and He could not take it, for His future was cast and His life was to be in the hands of the others who would soon arrive.

The one from the feast whose heart was dark approached with the soldiers, giving my dear one a kiss. They took Him away from the garden in the night, and I followed in a manner they could not observe.

The chosen ones had all fled, and now the Son stood alone.

He was led to one who wanted to remain the leader of the others, and His clothes were torn and He suffered.

The one whose heart was dark cast out the thirty pieces of silver that were given to him in exchange for finding the Son, then in sorrow he went to hang himself from a tree.

The leader asked my dear one if He was the King of the Jews, and the Son answered in a manner that confused them all the more.

All this I watched from the crowd as did the others gathered round. They knew not what I was, for I was now one of them in body.

They dragged a thief before the crowd, and the wife of the leader begged her husband to let my dear one go free.

But the words had been written and could not be changed.

The crowd called for the death of my beloved. The soldiers tore the clothes that the mother had made with her own hands, and then they made Him suffer.

They lay a scarlet robe around His shoulders, a crown of thorns upon His head, and a reed in His right hand.

The precious blood of the Son coursed down His brow.

I hid my face in shame for what was being done to Him.

The people around me, some who had not so long ago greeted Him with love and palms from the trees, now called for His death.

He, who I had watched grow from an infant, stood silently.

I stood in helplessness. I could not comfort Him.

My senses took on a new meaning. No longer did I smell the sweet scent of heaven, but the stink of bodies like mine that were all around.

No longer could I lift myself up in pure soul to the throne above, but stayed attached to the earth like a worm.

My feet felt the stones and dirt of the earth. I recoiled in horror from the look of hate on the faces of those around me.

Because the pain of remembering is so great, it has taken me until this time to write these words. But write I must, so that whoever may read this story will know of the Father and the Son.

And so I wept as I stood with the crowd, and the leader washed his hands of my dear one and gave Him over to the people.

Two lengths of wood, joined in the middle, were brought for Him to carry, and He was led out into the street. He walked through the people.

I ran, taking my place close to Him, and He saw that I was near.

His own tunic had been replaced on His body, and now it dragged in the mud as He walked in the street, carrying the wooden cross.

"Have strength," I whispered. "Bear this if you must, and know that I am by your side."

The crowd called out His name: "Jesus!" They threw sharp stones and spat upon Him. The dirty children followed their parents and threw small sticks and dirt.

As the blood continued running down into His eyes, His steps became unsteady and He fell forward. The weight of the cross crushed His back. The wounds opened, and pain contorted His face.

He glanced in my direction, and His face showed His words without speaking, *Where are you my friend? Do you see how I suffer? I feel I cannot bear it for long, but I have chosen this journey and now I must finish it.*

I am here, I answered silently, my eyes now filled with tears. *Be strong.*

Pulling himself to His feet, he stumbled on.

The mud mixed with the blood on His

robe and hair. As He walked, stones cut His feet. He turned the corner, and the crowd ran after Him, throwing stones and crying out.

His mother stood with her friends, and she looked upon her son with love. I followed His gaze as He found her in the crowd. Running to her side, I took my place near her and told her that I had been her child's guardian. She accepted me at once.

"I will stay with you until the end," I told her, "for I alone know what He has meant to you and I know your pain now as you look upon Him."

As my dear one struggled with the cross, the soldiers chose a man called Simon to help Him. The Father gave him blessings that day in eternity for his efforts.

He took the wood off my dear one's

shoulders and, placing it on his own back, dragged it through the mud.

On and on they walked, and now Simon, too, was stoned by the crowd. The people screamed and yelled, calling for my precious one's death.

The mother followed quietly, tears streaming down her face, and she wept for the years they had together and the pain of what was to be her son's fate.

A woman ran out to wipe my dear one's face, and the crowd tore her clothes for this and dragged her down into the street.

My precious one fell again, and wounds opened on His knees. The crown of thorns dug deeper into His flesh and into the bones of His skull. Blood flowed from His feet.

The deadly march came to a low hill, called Golgotha, the place of the Skull.

The soldiers ripped His robe from Him

and dragged Him to the cross where they pierced His hands and feet with spikes and nailed Him to the wood He had carried.

The leader had them put a title on the cross: Jesus of Nazareth. The King of the Jews.

They lifted the cross and crucified Him.

Now He saw His mother and one of His chosen few at His feet. While the soldiers drew lots for His seamless tunic, He said, "Woman behold your Son." To His friend He said, "Behold your mother."

His throat was parched and His lips dry so He said to the small crowd of soldiers, "I thirst!" One of them dipped a sponge in sour wine and put it to His mouth. When He received the wine, He said, "It is finished." Bowing His head He gave up His spirit to the Father.

The promise was fulfilled.

In that instant, dark clouds gathered overhead and violent rains came to the earth.

In that instant, dark clouds gathered overhead and violent rains came to the earth. Lightning cracked the sky through the dark, lighting the faces of each person watching His crucifixion. The soldiers grew fearful, and one pierced my dear one's side with his spear, insuring death. They cowered in the storm and the mother stood at the feet of the cross where I comforted her.

One of the soldiers dropped to his knees and wept tears of remorse for the death and for the pain my beloved suffered.

In the valley, the graves opened in the darkness and the molded bodies rose from their beds of death. The rain continued to lash our faces, and the lightning streaked around us.

We saw people running into the streets, crying out that the temple curtain had ripped from top to bottom.

The death of my beloved was noticed by the crowd. So it was that some now knew Him for who He was, and they lay in the mud, rain pouring on their backs, while they asked for forgiveness for their deeds.

The Great One looked upon those who repented with favor and granted that they would see His face in eternity.

So it ended.

My lord was dead, and the chaos of the city was complete.

There came a man, Joseph of Armithea, who received the body and together with Nicodemus bound my precious one in strips of linen anointed with spices. We hastened to a tomb Joseph had prepared so that the Son might be laid to rest before the Sabbath.

We watched while he gently placed the body in the tomb, and when we left a great stone was rolled across the entrance.

It was then that I turned to the women gathered round and knew that my destiny was to walk with them until death would claim their bodies and their souls be lifted to the heavens.

The women spent the next hours in great sorrow for the loss of the One whom they had come to love, but I kept watch for the next signs, which I knew would show His true spirit.

Early on the first day of the week, we all came to the tomb carrying spices and saw that the stone had been moved from its place.

My precious one's body was gone from the slab upon which it had lain. We consoled one another; the women feared that those who would do Him harm had removed Him.

The one called Mary Magdalene ran to

the friend of my Lord to tell them He was gone; Simon Peter chose to see the tomb for himself.

The great mystery of my precious one's origin was unfolding. I followed in silence and awe to where His friends gathered.

There the Son appeared, saying "Peace be with you." He showed them His wounds, proving, therefore, that He was their leader.

Those who were sure He was the same questioned not His appearance, and some had to be convinced. I knew He was one and the same who had been put to death.

He spent time with His friends, instructing them to carry on His work, and on the third day it came time for Him to return to His Father.

We gathered in a field near Bethany and heard His last words.

"Thus it is written and thus it was neces-

sary for the Christ to suffer and to rise from the dead on the third day, and that repentance and remission of sins should be preached in His name to all nations, beginning at Jerusalem.

"And you are witnesses to these things.

"Behold, I send the Promise of my Father upon you; but tarry in the city of Jerusalem until you are endued with power from on high."

As He spoke, a great radiance shone about as if the sky opened and the sun was in the heavens only for Him.

He was lifted from the ground slowly, drawn up through the clouds by the hand of the Great One himself. I saw around me that those who may have still had doubts about His heavenly origin now were of firm mind that He was of the Father.

By His act of rising from the dead and

returning to heaven He showed the world that He was the true Son of the Father.

I grieved for the loss of the sight of Him; yet I rejoiced, as did His friends, in our new duty as He directed.

I have carried out His wishes, and those of His Father, throughout the centuries, and I will continue to do so until the end of this world as we know it.

My existence has been one of joy in bringing His message to those who have sought truth in their lives. I have seen, too, the turmoil of the world caused by those who choose not to believe, or who have followed those who call themselves righteous but have darkened their hearts against the meaning of His spoken words.

These words of His life I now write so that others may read these words and be changed by the story of His life.

May His death and resurrection and the love of the Great One guide those who believe—in all that they do. One day they shall see His heavenly face and live in eternity in His sight.

That is what They wish and what my dear one has died for.

His death was not in vain. Rather, it is the salvation of the world.

Sara

January, 1832

The Journal Lives On

MANY YEARS HAVE passed since I first read the story of the journal to the mission children. My age and poor eyesight have caused me to look for another who will take up my duty.

As was true with me so long ago, there was one who has been prepared to receive the story. She now deserves the privilege of carrying on as a teacher where I cannot.

The sound of Charlotte's first footstep on my porch sets all of my senses on alert. The pot of fragrant jasmine tea is ready, and the front room is in order for my visitor.

Memories of our first meeting flash through my mind, ignoring twenty-four years of her growth.

I see her as a six-year-old again, snuggled comfortably against my side. I am reading to her and to the other children, noticing how she follows every word over my shoulder. Her silence strikes me as reverence and is a contrast to the constant shifting and whispering of my other small listeners.

That first year she moved wordlessly away from my chair at the end of the story and joined her mother. It struck me as slightly odd that she never asked me about the writer or the story. I had wanted to know about these things when I first heard it.

Some of the other children asked the questions I had expected, but not Charlotte.

At least not that year.

It wasn't until a few years later that she asked about the story.

She must have been ten the year she wanted to know if the tale was really true. I answered that it was a story that had been written in many forms and books, and its truths have served me well in my life.

When she asked about the truth of Sara's origin, I answered as my mother had, so many years ago: that we should concentrate on the message rather than the messenger.

Charlotte didn't return the next year. In fact, I didn't see her again until eight years after that, and when I did she had matured into a young woman of eighteen, a college freshman just beginning her own studies that would lead her to the same career I had pursued, a perfect choice for her caring, giving nature.

We had our first real conversation then, and she told me of her mother's death shortly after her last visit. She had spent the intervening years with an aunt who cared for her and didn't need the sort of charities we offered at the mission.

Why then had she returned, I asked her. Charlotte replied that she had come again to hear me read from the journal, for the story had inspired her to hold fast to her belief that she was worth the great sacrifice told on its pages.

She had endured the crushing loneliness of being an orphan at an early age and, as she said, she dearly wished for someone in her life to show her she was loved. Only the memory of the story carried her through to maturity and inspired her in making the decision to enter college.

When those treasured words came from her lips, I knew the time had come to turn the story over to her, and I let her read it to the youngsters gathered there for Easter.

She continued reading to them each year while I sat listening to the familiar tale. Somehow it took on a new meaning when I heard it in her voice, as if her suffering brought an understanding to the story that I never had.

She truly connected with the listeners and they with her. Their similar backgrounds bound them together, and I could see that the story took on a new meaning to them.

* * *

NOW IT IS time for her to carry on alone, for my age has finally set its limits and I find that I am confined to the boundaries of my home while the world goes on around me.

Charlotte's soft knock prompts my thoughts back to the present, and I move to the door in my steady, slow pace.

She is there with her first born, the child she has named Jonathan, which means "gift from God." Her husband is at home awaiting her return. They are hardly ever apart for more than a day.

I feel a slight twinge of sadness thinking that I have missed a man's devotion and love for a child in my life, but it passes swiftly.

She is there with her first born, the child she named Jonathan, which means "gift from God."

The words, *Charlotte, come in and sit down a moment and tell me exactly how you will carry on my work,* form in my mind, but I ask her to step inside and warm herself for a minute instead.

The cool March air has brought a chill to our skin as we stand in the doorway, and she accepts my hospitality and enters the front room.

She places her son's carrier on the floor and we embrace, holding each other for just a few moments longer than we ever have before.

"Thank you for believing enough in me to let me do your work for you," she says.

My smile belies my inner struggle and the temptation to turn back the clock so that this transition would not have to take place. I remember, again, her reverence for the journal and the changes the story brought to her life, and I summon the courage to release the book from my home.

"I always knew it would be you. From that first moment we met, I knew you thought of the journal the way I did. Do you remember that day?"

Charlotte sits on the couch, reaching for the tea in a familiar way, and I join her, waiting to hear her first impression of that meeting.

"When I first came to the mission, I was ashamed of our poverty. Everything about me seemed poor, even the clothes I wore. My mother and I were living in a tenement, and we walked miles to come to the Easter dinner. Even though I had her in my life, I felt a deep emptiness that I couldn't explain.

"When I heard the beautiful story told

in the words of Sara, I felt renewed in a way I have never been able to understand.

"It's that feeling that I want to convey to other children who will come to the mission. I only hope I can do it as well as you did."

I think of the sound of her voice as she has read the story in the past and the look of concentration and awe on her listeners' faces, and I reply, "You will do it better, Charlotte, for you were once one of them."

"I will never let the feeling I had when I came to the mission touch my son, of that you can be sure. I want more for him than that. For the children there I will give them the gift of the story, and hopefully they will find what I did in its pages," Charlotte says while she rocks the sleeping child. "And one day, when my son is old enough to understand, I will read it to him as well."

She takes a sip of tea and carefully places the cup back down on its saucer. She looks into my eyes for a moment and asks the question I had thought she would ask twenty-four years ago.

"Who was the writer—was Sara who I think she was?"

I had waited for this question, yet once asked, it comes as a surprise. "She was someone, or something, I suppose, who witnessed the events told in the journal. That is all I know, and it is all my own mother knew about her," I reply.

"Does she still walk the earth? Where is she today?" Charlotte asks.

"That is something I don't know. But I do know this—that whether you choose to believe in her is up to you. The value of the story lives on, even without her voice. I choose to believe that she was real.

There are things that have no explanation, and she is one of them," I answer slowly.

"Then I choose to believe as you do," she responds, reaching out to touch my shoulder with her slender hand. "Her journal will live on with me."

* * *

I FEEL AS if I have accomplished my life's work.

I have passed on something of benefit to the next generation, and that is all any of us can hope for.

Just as the death and resurrection of Jesus was part of his Father's plan for the salvation of the world, so is His plan for continuing the story of His son's life. Charlotte's appearance in my life was meant to be, and now I bow to this destiny, insuring the story will continue to reach others.

I think Sara would be pleased, knowing that her journal continues in the hands of another. Now you, too, can share her story as you wish.

About the Author

Maria I. Hodges is a graphic artist, illustrator, painter, and copywriter who has worked in the Atlanta metropolitan area for more than twenty years. The mother of one son, whom she says allows her to know what it means to love without reservation, she draws on her experience as a mother in creating this story of the intense love and protection of Sara for the Christ Child. Maria lives in Stone Mountain, Georgia.